Weekly Reader Children's Book Club Presents

# Curious George Flies a Kite

## MARGRET REY

Pictures by
## H. A. REY

HOUGHTON MIFFLIN COMPANY BOSTON

This book is a presentation of Newfield Publications, Inc.
Newfield Publications offers book clubs for children
from preschool through high school. For further
information write to: **Newfield Publications, Inc.,**
4343 Equity Drive, Columbus, Ohio 43228.

Published by arrangement with Houghton Mifflin Company.
Newfield Publications is a federally registered
trademark of Newfield Publications, Inc.
Weekly Reader is a federally registered trademark
of Weekly Reader Corporation.

[ISBN: 0-395-16965-8]

This is George.

He lives in the house

of the man with the yellow hat.

George is a little monkcy,

and all monkeys are curious.

But no monkey

is as curious as George.

That is why his name is

Curious George.

"I have to go out now,"
said the man with the yellow hat.
"Be a good little monkey
till I come back.
Have fun and play
with your new ball,
but do not be too curious."
And the man went out.

It was
a lot of fun
for George
to play with
his big new ball.
The ball
went up,
and George
went up,

and the ball
went down,
and George
went down.

George could
do a lot of tricks
with his ball too.
This was one
of the tricks.
He could get up
on the ball like this.

Or do it this way,
with his head down.

This was
another trick
George could do.
He could hold
the ball on his head,
like this.

Look—no hands.
What a good trick!
But—but where did the ball go?

George ran after it.
The ball had gone
into another room.

There was
a big window
in the room.

George liked to look
out of that window.

He could see
a lot from there.

He let the ball go
and looked out.

George
could see
Bill on his bike
and the lake
with a boat
on it.

George
could see
a big house
in a little garden
and a little house
in a big garden.

The big house
was the house
where Bill lived.

But who lived
in the little house?
George was curious.
Who could live in a house
that was so little?

George had to find out,
so he went to the big garden.

The garden had a high wall,
but not too high
for a monkey.

George got up on the wall.

All he had to do now
was jump down—
so George jumped down
into the big garden.

Now he could take a good look
at the little house.

And what did he see?

A big white bunny
and a lot of little bunnies.

George looked and looked and looked.

Bunnies were something new to him.

How funny they were!

The big bunny
was Mother Bunny.

She was as big as George.

But the little bunnies were so little
that George could hold
one of them in his hand,
and that is what he wanted to do.

How could he get a bunny
out of the house?

A house must have a door
to get in and to get out.

But where was the door
to the bunny house?

Oh—there it was!

George put his hand in
and took out
a baby bunny.

What fun it was
to hold a baby bunny!
And the bunny did not mind.
It sat in his hand,
one ear up and one ear down
and looked at George,
and George looked back at it.

17

Now he and the bunny
could play in the garden.

They could play a game.

They could play Get the Bunny.

George would let the bunny hop away,
and then he would run after it
and get it back.

George put the bunny down.

Then he looked away.

One—two—run!

The bunny was off like a shot.

George did not look.

Now he had to wait a little.

One—two—three—four—he waited.

Then George looked up.
Where was the bunny?
He could not see it.
Where was it?
Where had it gone?

George looked for it here,
and he looked for it there.
He could not find it.

Where was the bunny?

It could not get

out of the garden.

It could not get up the wall

the way George could.

It could not fly away.

It had to be here—

but it was not.

The bunny was gone,

and all the fun

was gone too.

George sat down.

He had been a bad little monkey.

Why was he so curious?

Why did he let the bunny go?

Now he could not put it
back into the bunny house
where it could be
with Mother Bunny.

Mother Bunny—George looked up.

Why, that was it!

Mother Bunny could help him!

George got up.

He had to have some string.

Maybe there was some in the garden.

Yes, there was a string

and a good one too.

George took the string

and went back

to the bunny house.

Mother Bunny

was at the door.

George let her out

and put the string on her.

And Mother Bunny knew what to do.

Away she went
with her head down
and her ears up.

All George could do was
hold the string
and run after her.

And then Mother Bunny sat down.

She saw something,

and George saw it too.

Something white

that looked like a tail,

like the tail of the baby bunny.

And that is what it was!

But where was the rest of the bunny?

It was down in a hole.

A bunny likes to dig a hole
and then go down and live in it.

But this bunny was too little
to live in a hole.

It should live in a bunny house.

So George got hold
of the little white tail
and pulled the baby bunny out.

Then they all ran back
to the bunny house.

George did not have to put a string
on the baby bunny.

It ran after its mother
all the way home.

George took the string
off Mother Bunny
and helped them back
into the house.

Then Mother Bunny

and all the little ones

lay down to sleep.

George looked at them.

It was good to see the baby bunny

back where it should be.

And now George would go

back to where he should be.

When he came to the wall,
he could see something funny
in back of it.

George got up on the wall
to find out what it was.

He saw
a long string
on a long stick.
A fat man
had the long stick
in his hand.
What could the man do
with a stick that long?
George was curious.

The fat man was
on his way to the lake,
and soon George was
on his way to the lake too.

The man took a hook
out of his box,
put it on a string
and then put something on the hook.

Then the man let the string
down into the water
and waited.

Now George knew!
The string on the stick
was to fish with.

When the man pulled the string
out of the water,
there was a big fish on the hook.

George saw the man
pull one fish after another
out of the lake,
till he had
all the fish
he wanted.

What fun
it must be to fish!

George wanted to fish too.

He had his string.

All he needed was a stick,

and he knew where to get that.

George ran home as fast as he could.

In the kitchen
he took the mop
off the kitchen wall.

The mop would make
a good stick.

Now George had the string and the stick.

He was all set to fish.

Or was he?

Not yet.

George had to have a hook
and on the hook something
that fish like to eat.

Fish would like cake,
and George knew where to find some.

But where could he get a hook?

Why—there was a hook
for the mop on the kitchen wall!

It would have
to come out.

With the hook
on the string
and the string
on the stick
and the cake
in the box
in his hand,
George went back
to the lake.

George sat down,

put some cake on the hook,

and let the line down into the water.

Now he had to wait,

just as the man had waited.

George was curious.

The fish were curious too.

All kinds of fish came

to look at the line,

big fish and little fish,

fat fish and thin fish,

red fish and yellow fish

and blue fish.

One of them was near the hook.

The cake was just what he wanted.

George sat and waited.

Then the line shook.

There must be a fish on the hook.

George pulled the line up.

The cake was gone,

but no fish was on the hook.

Too bad!

George put more cake on the hook.

Maybe this time

he would get a fish.

But no!

The fish just took the cake

off the hook

and went away.

Well, if George
could not get the fish,
the fish would not get the cake.
George would eat it.
He liked cake too.
He would find another way
to get a fish.

George looked into the water.

That big red one there
with the long tail!

It was so near,
maybe he could get it
with his hands.

George got down
as low as he could,
and put out his hand.

SPLASH!

Into the lake he went!

The water was cold and wet
and George was cold and wet too.
This was no fun at all.

When he came out of the water,
Bill was there with his kite.

"My, you are wet!" Bill said.

"I saw you fall in,
so I came to help you get out.

Too bad you did not get a fish!

But it is good the fish
did not get you."

"Now I can show you how high
my kite can fly," Bill went on.

Bill put his bike up near a tree
and then they ran off.

There was a lot of wind that day,
and that was just what they needed.
The wind took the kite up fast.
George was too little
to hold it in this wind.

A kite that big
could fly away with him.
So Bill had to hold it.
George saw the kite
go up and up and up.
What fun it was to fly a kite!

They let the kite fly
for a long time
till Bill said,
   "I will get the kite down now.
   I must go home
and you should too."
   But when Bill pulled the string in,
the kite got into the top
of a high tree.
   Bill could not get it down.

"Oh, my fine new kite!
I can not let go of it.
I must have it back,"
Bill said.
"But the tree
is too high for me."

But no tree
was too high for George.
He went up to the top
in no time.

Then, little by little,
he got the string
out of the tree.

Down he came
with the kite
and gave it back
to Bill.

"Thank you, George, thanks a lot,"
Bill said. "I am so happy
to have the kite back.

Now you may have
a ride home on my bike.

I will run back to the lake
and get it.

You wait here for me
with the kite,
but do not let it fly away."

George looked at the kite.

Then he took the string in his hand.

He knew he could not fly the kite
in this wind,
but maybe he could let it
go up just a little bit.

George was curious.

He let the string go a little,
and then a little more,
and then a little more,
and then a little more.

When Bill came back,
there was no kite
and there was no George.
"George!" he called.
"Where are you?"

Then he looked up.

There they were,

way up in the sky!

Bill had to get help fast.

He would go to the man

with the yellow hat.

The man would know

what to do.

"George is not here,"
said the man with the yellow hat
when Bill came.

"Have you seen him?"

"George and my kite
are up in the sky
near the lake," Bill shouted.

"I came to . . ."

But the man did not wait

to hear any more.

He ran to his car and jumped in.

"I will get him back," he said.

"I must get George back."

All this time
the wind took the kite up
and George with it.

It was fun
to fly about in the sky.

But when George looked down,
the fun was gone.

He was up so high
that all the big houses
looked as little as bunny houses.

George did not like it a bit.

He wanted to get down, but how?

Not even a monkey
can jump from the sky.
George was scared.
What if he never got back?
Maybe he would fly
on and on and on.
Oh, he would never, never
be so curious again,
if just this one time
he could find a way to get home.

Hummmmm—hummmmm.

What was that?

George could hear something,

and then he saw something

fly in the sky just like a kite.

It was a helicopter,

and in the helicopter,

hurrah,

was the man with the yellow hat!

Down from
the helicopter
came a long line.

George got hold of it,
and the man with the yellow hat
pulled him up.

George held on to the kite,
for he had to give it back to Bill.

"I am so happy
to have you back, George,"
said the man with the yellow hat.

"I was scared,
and you must have been scared too.

I know you will not want
to fly a kite again
for a long, long time.

You must give it back to Bill
when we get home."

72

"Hurrah!" Bill shouted
when George came
to give him the kite.
"George is back,
and my kite is back too!"

And then Bill
took George by the hand
and went with him
into the little garden,

and from the little garden

into the big garden,

where the bunny house was.

"Here is one of my baby bunnies,"
Bill said.

"Take it, it is for you!"

A baby bunny for George!

George took it in his hands

and held it way up.

It was HIS bunny now.

He could take it home with him.

And that is
what he
did.